PICTUE
THO

Mimi's Tutu

by
Tynia Thomassie

illustrated by
Jan Spivey Gilchrist

SCHOLASTIC INC. / New York

GLOSSARY

lapa — LAH · puh — decorative piece of cloth worn as a wrap-around skirt

FEMALE NAMES

M'bewe — m · BAY · way

Iecine — ee · SEEN

Magalee — mah · gah · LEE

INSTRUMENTS

claves — CLAH · ves — two wooden sticks

shekere — SHAKE · eh · ray — beaded hollow gourd

djembe — JIM · BAY — drum

A special thanks to Dahoue Mamadou, Pat Hall-Smith, Osunwale Lett, Kevin Burrell, and Sarah Wendt for our time together. And always, glories to my Dave, Matthew, and Will.

— T.T.

Thank you to Dania Monique Leggans.

— J.S.G.

Cataloging-in-Publication Data available
Library of Congress number: 94-33022
ISBN 0-590-44020-9

12 11 10 9 8 7 6 5 4 3 2 1   6 7 8 9/9 0/0
Printed in Singapore   46
First printing, February 1996
The illustrations in this book were executed
in watercolor and pastel on illustration board.
Production supervision by Angela Biola
Designed by Claire Counihan

To every child
whose spirit has been freed
by dance and percussion
— T.T.

To Lewis and Joanne Koch,
for your work and dedication
to children
— J.S.G.

When MIMI was born, she followed a long line of boys. The family rejoiced at the arrival of their first little girl. Especially the grandmothers.

All the grandfathers and uncles had been honored with namesakes. There was Jacques, for Mama's father, and Emile after Mama's brother. Clarence and Forest were named for Daddy's father and brother. In fact, there were more boys than uncles and grandfathers to name them after.

Now, all the grandmothers and aunts felt that the new baby should be named after *them*. But, there were two grandmothers and two aunts, and only one very small little girl.

That's how she came to be called M'bewe Iecine Magalee Isabella . . . or MIMI for short.

From the time MIMI was a baby, she was always surrounded by music and dance. This was her family's tradition. Grampa Jacques beat out rhythms on the *congas*, while Uncle Forest played the cowbell. Aunt Isabella played the *claves* and Gramma Iecine shook the brightly beaded *shekere*.

Gramma M'bewe knew the ceremonial dances of Guinea, and Mama was a fine dancer, too.

Whenever the family gathered, everyone from the tallest to the smallest grabbed an instrument or danced.

MIMI would bob to the beat or shake her rattle in time to the music.

As MIMI grew older, Mama decided to return to her African dance class.

MIMI loved to go along with Mama. The *djembe* drums would roll, and all the ladies would leap and sway in their multicolored skirts.

"The skirts are actually wraps of cloth called *lapas*," Mama explained.

"*Lapas!*" MIMI repeated, as she watched from the corner.

When MIMI had been especially good, Mama would take her hand, and they would dance, side by side across the floor.

MIMI would whisk her arms up and jump and shake. All the other ladies smiled in approval.

"Why, what a fine dancer you are, Miss MIMI," one woman said. "You're carrying on your family's tradition."

MIMI liked that.

One day, a new dancer named Natasha came to class. She brought her daughter Sophie, who looked about MIMI's age.

Sophie wore one bright yellow sock and one bright red sock. Her shoes had pink shoelaces. She had blue and yellow ribbons in her hair. And even though there was a special corner of the room where all the children sat, Sophie made it clear that *she* did not intend to sit.

Sophie was going to dance with her mother during the entire class!

But that wasn't all.

Sophie reached into her beautifully embroidered bag and pulled out a pale green tutu, just like ballerinas wear. She slipped it over her head and adjusted it at her waist.

Everyone stared at Sophie. She was a blaze of color.

"Look at her in that tutu!" laughed MIMI's friend, Jennifer. "She thinks it's a ballet class."

MIMI glanced down at her plain shirt and shorts.

"She looks pretty to me," said MIMI.

MIMI studied Sophie's every move.
"She's only fair," MIMI muttered.
Sophie leaped by.
MIMI mumbled, "Okay . . . she can dance."

When Mama held out her hand for MIMI to join her on the dance floor, MIMI did not feel the usual skip in her heart.

But the drums beat away her small thoughts. As her feet stomped in time to the music, MIMI began to feel good again.

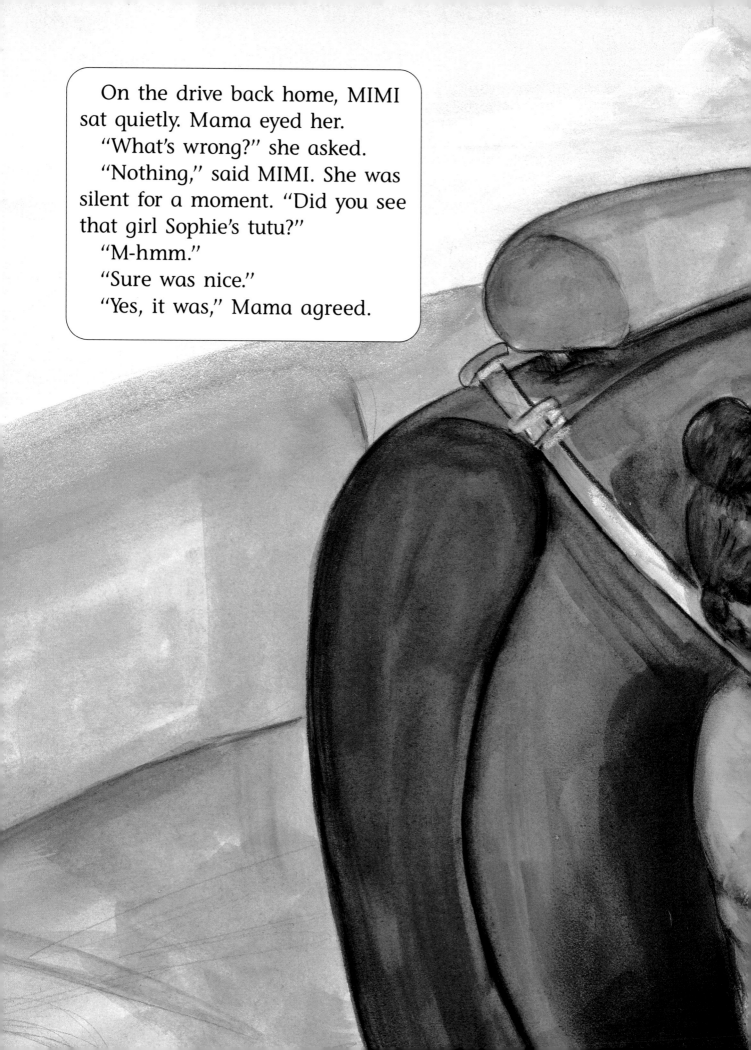

On the drive back home, MIMI
sat quietly. Mama eyed her.
"What's wrong?" she asked.
"Nothing," said MIMI. She was
silent for a moment. "Did you see
that girl Sophie's tutu?"
"M-hmm."
"Sure was nice."
"Yes, it was," Mama agreed.

That evening, everyone noticed that MIMI seemed unhappy. MIMI watched her grandmothers and aunts huddle with Mama, but she didn't care. She just thought about Sophie and her tutu.

The next Saturday, before Mama and MIMI were supposed to leave for dance class, MIMI found Gramma M'bewe and her aunts waiting for her in the kitchen.

"We understand you've been yearning for a tutu," Gramma M'bewe said.

"Maybe," whispered MIMI. She stared hard at the floor.

"Look up, MIMI," said Gramma M'bewe.

In her hands, she held a beautiful *lapa*. It had a specially designed belt of beige cowrie shells, and beads of black, orange, and dark green. When it shook, it sounded just like Gramma Iecine's *shekere*. And, it was *exactly* MIMI's size!

"This is a skirt that suits *you*, M'bewe Iecine Magalee Isabella," said Gramma M'bewe. "You'll celebrate your ancestry when you dance in it, child."

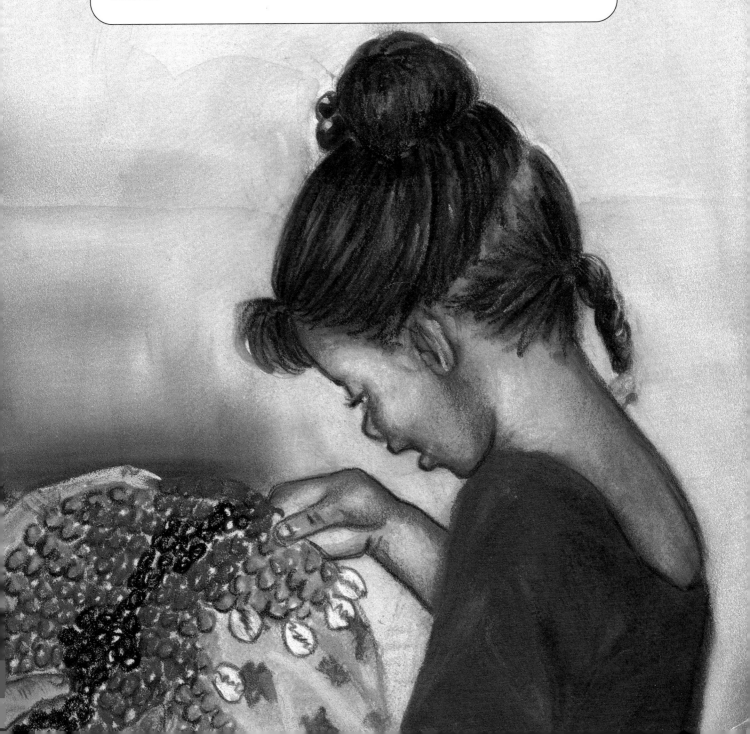

That day, Mama told MIMI that she could take the whole dance class.

MIMI beamed. She tucked her *lapa* about her waist and patted her cowrie shell belt.

Sophie whispered, "I love your skirt."

"Thank you," glowed MIMI. "I love your skirt, too."

The two little girls shared a smile as the drums popped the air.

MIMI sparkled in her *lapa* and belt — her very own kind of tutu. She danced as if her heart lived in her feet, proud to carry on her family's tradition.